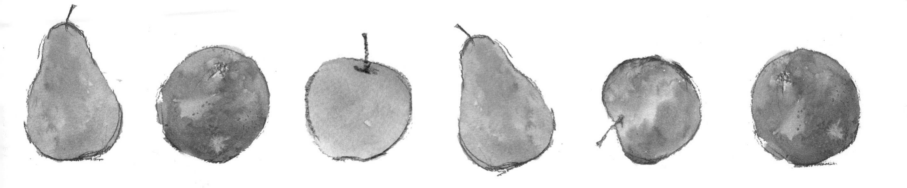

Orange
Pear
Apple
Bear

For Mik

www.twohootsbooks.com

First
published in 2006
by Macmillan Children's
Books. This edition published
2016 by Two Hoots, an
imprint of Pan Macmillan, 20
New Wharf Road, London N1 9RR
Associated companies throughout
the world. www.panmacmillan.com
ISBN 978-1-5098-3662-8
Text and illustrations copyright
© Emily Gravett 2006
The right of Emily Gravett to be identified
as the author and illustrator of this work has
been asserted by her in accordance with the
Copyright, Designs and Patents Act 1988. All rights
reserved. No part of this publication may be
reproduced, stored in a retrieval system, or
transmitted, in any form or by any means
(electronic, mechanical, photocopying,
recording or otherwise), without the prior
written permission of the publisher. Pan
Macmillan does not have any control over,
or any responsibility for, any author or third
party websites referred to in or on this book.
A CIP catalogue record for this book is avail-
able from the British Library. Printed in China. The
illustrations in this book were created using pencil,
watercolour and five carefully chosen words.
1 3 5 7 9 8 6 4 2

Orange
Pear
Apple
Bear

Emily Gravett

TWO HOOTS

Orange

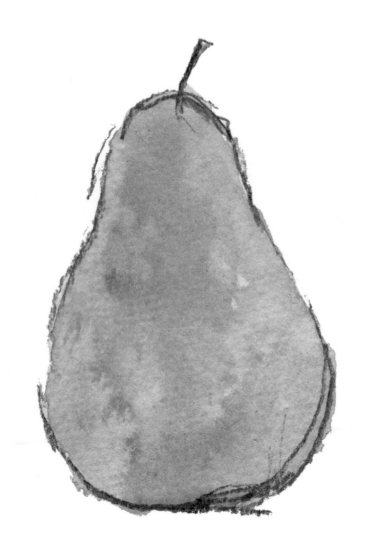

Pear

Apple

Bear

Apple, pear

Orange bear

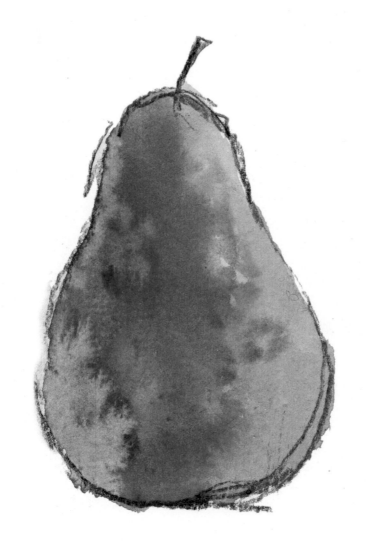

Orange pear

Apple bear

Apple, orange, pear bear

Orange, pear, apple, bear

Apple,

bear,

orange,

pear

Orange, bear

Pear, bear

Apple, bear

There!

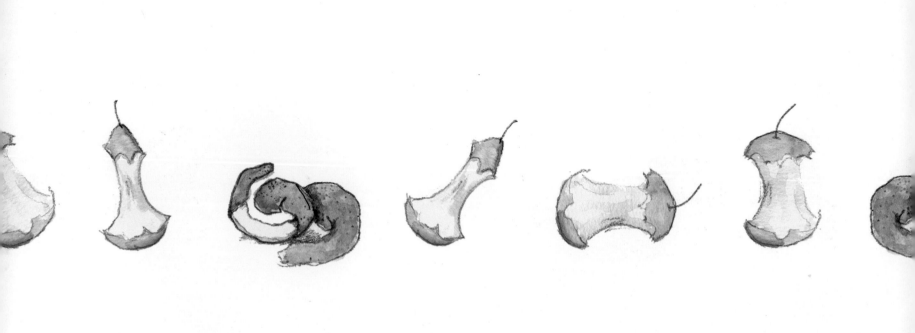

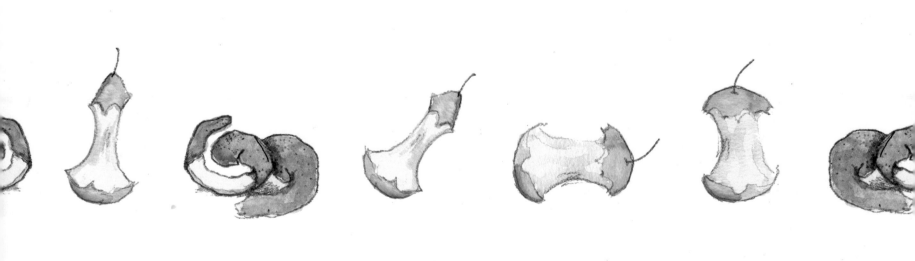

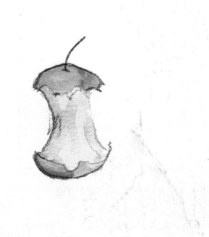